ISBN: 1-903078-48-2

www.siphano.com

Colour separation: Vivliosynergatiki, Athens, Greece
Printed in Italy by Grafiche AZ, Verona

Three Wishes, Master Dog

Gianluca Garofalo

SIPHANO PICTURE BOOKS • LONDON

Dog was playing in the fields when he came across a strange green bottle. It smelled old and mouldy, not like anything Dog had ever known before. Dog pulled the cork out with his teeth.

What could be in the bottle?

It looked empty at first, but soon wisps of blue smoke started to creep from its neck...

The bottle began to hiss and the blue smoke grew thicker and thicker until... out popped a genie! It was a boy genie dressed in a crisp silk outfit and carrying a magic stick.

"You have released me from my bottle, Master Dog," said the genie. "Now I can grant you three wishes, and then I shall be free."

Dog only answered with a bark, but the genie didn't want to waste time: "Well then, I'll just have to give Master Dog the usual wishes," he thought.

He waved his magic stick...

...and made Dog a smart set of clothes.
Dog found himself wearing a flannel suit
with a silk tie and a bowler hat. The pockets
were filled with pens and notebooks and
all sorts of bits and pieces. He even had
a gold watch on a chain.

"What shall I do with all these fancy clothes?"
wondered Dog. "They are so uncomfortable."

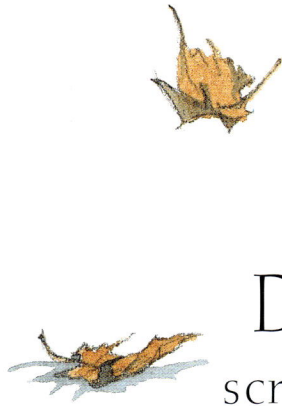

Dog wriggled and scratched and rolled on the ground. He had to get out of the clothes.

Eventually he ran to the duck pond. He dived in and swam and splashed in the water until all his handsome clothes came off.

"Master Dog doesn't care for fashionable clothes," thought the genie.

Dog was just about to start playing with the ducks when the genie swished his stick through the air for the second time...

... and made Dog a sumptuous feast! There in the farmyard stood a grand table piled high with rich delicacies, tasty morsels and delicious puddings, all served on precious bone china.

Dog sniffed everything thoroughly, but nothing was quite to his taste... except for the two old bones lying on the ground.

Dog took one of the bones and carried it off
to chew while the other animals helped themselves
to the genie's fine cuisine.

"Master Dog doesn't like good food, either,"
thought the genie. He swooshed his stick through
the air for the third and last time...

... and made Dog a palace fit for a king!
It was a splendid palace built of marble
with elegant sculptures, golden
decorations and a royal crest above
the door.

"Surely Master Dog will appreciate
this," thought the genie.

Dog climbed the stairs
and pushed open the door.

He looked around the palace, and found
a great princely bed. The pillows were beautifully
emroidered and the linen was scented with lavender.

Dog climbed up for a rest, but he wasn't used
to sleeping on anything quite so soft...

...so he ran off to the stable to find his friend
the cow. He squeezed in next to her on a pile of hay
and closed his eyes for a quick snooze.

This was too much for the poor genie.

"Master Dog doesn't like anything I make for him," he thought sadly. "What use is it being a genie if I can't make my master happy?"

He was sitting feeling sorry for himself when Dog bounded back outside. He had woken up from his nap, and was looking for someone to play with.

Dog saw a stick that was perfect for playing fetch.
He grabbed the stick, rushed over and jumped
on the genie, wagging his tail excitedly.

"Do you want to play fetch, Master Dog?" asked
the genie in surprise. "Well... why not!"

The genie put down his own magic stick and took off his special outfit. Underneath, he was wearing clothes which were not so fancy, but they were much more comfortable for running around on the farm.

He threw the stick high into the air and Dog jumped up to catch it. Dog brought it back and the genie threw it again and again, until at last they were both out of breath.

"How wonderful life is here on the farm, Master Dog!" confessed the genie after a while. "Now that I'm free I have a wish of my own: I wish to stay here with you forever."

Then the genie took Dog in his arms, and they thought of all the games they could play together. They were happy to have become such good friends.